Unsolved!

MYSTERIES OF GIANT HUMANLIKE CREATURES

Kathryn Walker

based on original text by Brian Innes

UNSOLVED · UNSOLVED ·

Crabtree Publishing Company

www.crabtreebooks.com

Crabtree Publishing Company
www.crabtreebooks.com

Author: Kathryn Walker
based on original text by Brian Innes
Project editor: Kathryn Walker
Picture researcher: Rachel Tisdale
Managing editor: Miranda Smith
Art director: Jeni Child
Design manager: David Poole
Editorial director: Lindsey Lowe
Children's publisher: Anne O'Daly
Editor: Molly Aloian
Proofreaders: Adrianna Morganelli, Crystal Sikkens
Project coordinator: Robert Walker
Production coordinator: Katherine Berti
Prepress technicians: Margaret Amy Salter, Katherine Berti

This edition published in 2009 by
Crabtree Publishing Company

The Brown Reference Group plc
First Floor
9-17 St. Albans Place
London N1 0NX
www.brownreference.com

Photographs:
Corbis: Bettmann: p. 15;
Marc Charuel/Sygma: p. 27
Fortean Picture Library: p. 4–5, 7 (right), 8, 9, 13, 18, 19, 21, 23 (top right), 25, 30
Istockphoto: Stuart Murchison: p. 12;
Klaus Nilkens: p. 28
Mary Evans Picture Library: p. 14
Shutterstock: Mike Flippo: p. 20;
Tracy Hardy: p. 10–11;
Lindsay Noechel: p. 7 (left);
Stephen Rudolf: p. 16–17;
Igor Smichkov: p. 22–23;
Yan Zenkis: p. 24
TopFoto: National Pictures: cover

Illustration:
Stefan Chabluk: p. 29

Every effort has been made to trace the owners of copyrighted material.

Library and Archives Canada Cataloguing in Publication

Walker, Kathryn, 1957-
Mysteries of giant humanlike creatures / Kathryn Walker ; based on original text by Brian Innes.

(Unsolved!)
Includes index.
ISBN 978-0-7787-4143-5 (bound).--ISBN 978-0-7787-4156-5 (pbk.)

1. Yeti--Juvenile literature. 2. Sasquatch--Juvenile literature. 3. Wild men--Juvenile literature. I. Innes, Brian II. Title. III. Series: Unsolved! (St. Catharines, Ont.)

QL89.2.Y4W34 2008 j001.944 C2008-904324-3

Library of Congress Cataloging-in-Publication Data

Walker, Kathryn.
Mysteries of giant humanlike creatures / Kathryn Walker ; based on original text by Brian Innes.
p. cm. -- (Unsolved!)
Includes index.
ISBN-13: 978-0-7787-4156-5 (pbk. : alk. paper)
ISBN-10: 0-7787-4156-7 (pbk. : alk. paper)
ISBN-13: 978-0-7787-4143-5 (reinforced library binding : alk. paper)
ISBN-10: 0-7787-4143-5 (reinforced library binding : alk. paper)
1. Yeti--Juvenile literature. 2. Sasquatch--Juvenile literature. 3. Wild men--Juvenile literature. I. Innes, Brian. II. Title. III. Series.

QL89.2.Y4W34 2009
001.944--dc22

2008030073

Crabtree Publishing Company
www.crabtreebooks.com 1-800-387-7650

Published in Canada
Crabtree Publishing
616 Welland Ave.
St. Catharines, Ontario
L2M 5V6

Published in the United States
Crabtree Publishing
PMB 59051
350 Fifth Avenue, 59th Floor
New York, New York 10118

Printed in Canada/042011/KR20110304

Contents

A Startling Sight

...In 1967, a humanlike beast was caught on film in northern California.

On October 20, 1967, Roger Patterson and his friend Bob Gimlin were in northern California. They were riding their horses through a forest alongside Bluff Creek.

Suddenly, the men saw a huge, hairy figure stand up. It was on the other side of the creek. Patterson grabbed his movie camera and began to film it. The creature turned to look at him. Then it disappeared into the **undergrowth**.

The film that Patterson took ran for about one minute. It was jumpy and not very clear. But it did show a big female creature. She looked something like a gorilla. The men claimed they had taken the first moving pictures of the creature known as Bigfoot.

How Strange...

- The creature left huge footprints in the dirt. The men made **plaster casts** of the footprints.
- The footprints were about 14 inches (35.5 cm) long and 5 inches (12.7 cm) wide.
- The creature's single step was about 40 inches (102 cm) long.

>> **undergrowth** — Bushes and plants growing under trees

"The creature turned to look at him. Then it disappeared into the undergrowth."

This picture is a still from the film that Patterson took of Bigfoot in 1967. Some people thought the film was a fake.

>> **plaster cast** — Model made by pouring liquid plaster into a mold and letting it harden

Bigfoot of North America

...Bigfoot is perhaps the most famous giant humanlike beast.

There are stories of wild humanlike creatures living in different parts of the world. The creature said to live in North America is known as Bigfoot. Canadians call it the Sasquatch. This name comes from a Native American word for "hairy giant."

Native Americans have told stories of Bigfoot for centuries. Bigfoot is said to be tall and covered with reddish-black hair. It walks upright and gets its name from the huge footprints that it leaves behind.

Bigfoot is said to live in **remote** forests. Most sightings of the creature have been in the wild country of northwestern United States or in British Columbia, Canada.

How Strange...

- Scientist Grover Krantz collected more than 1,000 reports of Bigfoot sightings. He thought that half of these could have been true.
- In July 1884, one newspaper said that a large, apelike beast had been captured in British Columbia. Many people now think this story was a **hoax**.

>> **remote** — A long way from cities or towns

"Bigfoot is said to be tall and covered with reddish-black hair."

This is an artist's idea of what Bigfoot, or the Sasquatch, looks like. Many people have reported seeing the creature in the forests of British Columbia (left).

>> **hoax** — A trick

In 1924, a Canadian named Albert Ostman had a frightening experience. But Ostman did not tell his story for 33 years. He had worried that people would think he was crazy.

Kidnapped by the Bigfoot

Ostman was a **logger**. In the summer of 1924, he said he had been camping near Toba Inlet. This is a bay opposite from Vancouver Island in Canada. One night, he woke up to find himself being carried. He was still inside his sleeping bag.

The man on the right in this picture is Albert Ostman. In 1957, Ostman told the story of how he had been ***kidnapped*** *by a Bigfoot.*

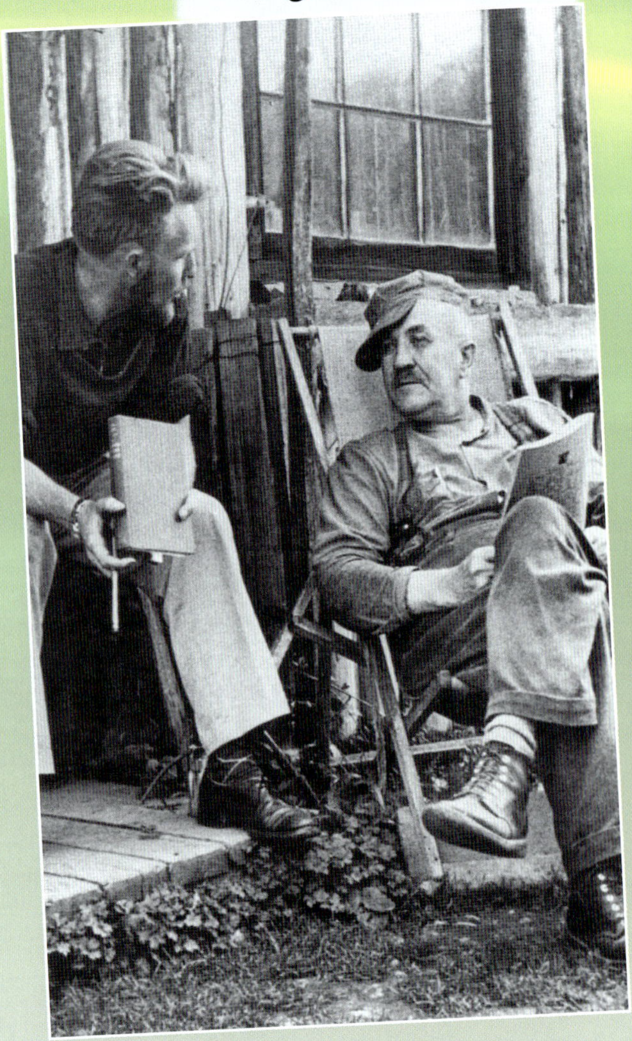

Ostman was then dumped on the ground. He found himself in the middle of a Bigfoot family. There was a mother, father, son, and daughter. The father was the tallest. He was about 8 feet (2.5 m) tall. All four creatures were covered in hair.

Ostman said that the bigfoot family kept him prisoner for six days. During the day, the females would search for food. The males stayed to keep watch on Ostman. Finally, he managed to escape.

>> **kidnapped** — Taken away by force

This is a photograph of Roger Patterson. It was taken hours after he filmed the Bigfoot. Patterson is holding plaster casts of the huge footprints made by the creature.

Bluff Creek

In 1958, workers in the Bluff Creek region of northern California kept finding huge footprints. The footprints circled around heavy equipment that the workers were using. The men made casts of the footprints.

In 1967, Patterson filmed the Bigfoot in this same area (see page 4). At first, many people said that Patterson's film was a hoax. They thought it showed a man in a gorilla suit.

Some Russian scientists also studied the film. The scientists decided that the creature could not be human. They said it moved too fast.

"...people said that Patterson's film was a hoax."

>> **logger** — A person who cuts down trees

The Yeti

...There are stories of a giant beast living in the Himalaya Mountains.

The Himalaya Mountains stretch along the northeastern **border** of India. Some of the highest **peaks** in the world are in the Himalayas.

N. A. Tombazi was a Greek photographer. In spring, 1925, he was with a group of climbers in the Himalayas. Suddenly, a guide pointed to a spot about 900 feet (275 m) away.

Tombazi looked and saw a figure walking upright. It looked as if it was naked. Tombazi watched the figure disappear into the bushes.

Later, Tombazi returned to the spot. He found footprints in the snow. Their shape was like those of a man, but they were only six to seven inches (15–18 cm) long. Many people said that Tombazi had seen the creature known locally as the "yeti."

>> **border** — A boundary or line that separates two countries or regions

"Some of the highest peaks in the world are in the Himalayas."

These are the snow-topped Himalaya Mountains. People sometimes call them "the roof of the world." Could they be home to giant humanlike creatures?

>> **peak** —The pointed top of a mountain or ridge

Mount Everest is the highest peak in the Himalayas. It is also the highest mountain on Earth. Everest lies on the border between the countries of Tibet and Nepal. People living on its lower slopes are known as Sherpas.

The animals in this picture are a type of cattle known as ***yaks****. Some Tibetan farmers say yetis have killed their yaks for food.*

The Abominable Snowman

Sherpas believe that a strange creature lives in the Himalayas. They call the creature the *yeh-teh*, or yeti. It is said tolive in the areas where trees do not grow and there is always snow.

Sherpas say the yeti is about the size of a human. It walks on two legs and has long arms. Reddish hair covers its body and it has a pointed head. Sometimes, the yeti come down the mountain to steal food from villages.

"A huge yeti picked up the captain and carried him off to a cave."

>> **yak** — A long-haired ox found in Tibet and central Asia

In the 1920s, a British explorer heard his Sherpa guides talk about the yeti as *metoh-kangmi*. It was a term that Sherpas used to describe any mountain beast.

Later, *metoh-kangmi* was incorrectly translated into English as "Abominable Snowman." This name soon became another name for the yeti. The word "abominable" means "very unpleasant" or "causing disgust."

This picture shows what the yeti or Abominable Snowman might look like.

Saved by a Yeti

In 1938, French-born Captain d'Auvergne told a strange story. He had been traveling alone in the Himalayas. The captain became exhausted, cold, and almost **snow-blind**.

A huge yeti picked up the captain and carried him off to a cave. The yeti was nearly 9 feet (3 m) tall. Captain d'Auvergne said that the creature fed and cared for him until he was able to walk again.

>> **snow-blind** — Blinded for a short time by the brightness of sunlight on snow

A Tale of Two Yetis

Slavomir Rawicz was a Polish soldier. During World War II, he was captured by the Russians. In 1942, Rawicz and six others managed to escape. Rawicz claimed that they then walked thousands of miles and crossed the Himalayas into India. On the way, they saw two huge yetis.

Rawicz said that the yetis were nearly 8 feet (2.5 m) tall. Their heads were square-shaped and they had sloping shoulders.

The group of men watched the creatures for about two hours. Rawicz said that the yetis did not seem interested in the humans.

How Strange...

- In 1951, climbers Eric Shipton and Michael Ward found some large footprints on Mount Everest.
- Shipton took photographs of one footprint. It was nearly 13 inches (33 cm) long and 8 inches (20 cm) wide.

This is a photograph taken by Eric Shipton in 1951. It shows a footprint found in the Himalayas. The ***ice ax*** *gives an idea of its size.*

>> **ice ax** — An ax used by mountaineers for cutting footholds in ice

The man on the left of this picture is Tenzing Norgay. Edmund Hillary is on the right. The two men reached the top of Everest on May 29, 1953.

On Top of the World

In 1953, Edmund Hillary from New Zealand and Tenzing Norgay from Nepal made history. They became the first men to stand on the **summit** of Mount Everest. Hillary and Norgay reported seeing yeti footprints on Everest.

Norgay claimed that he had often seen similar footprints. He also told Hillary that his father had once been chased down a slope by a yeti.

>> **summit** — The highest point of a mountain

Wildman of China

...A large, humanlike creature is said to live in the forests of China.

Early in 1976, some Chinese loggers were traveling in their truck. They were going down a dirt road through a forest. The men had been working in the mountains of Hubei Province. This is a wild area in the **valley** of the Chang (Yangtze) River.

Suddenly, the men saw a large, hairy figure. It was standing in the middle of the dirt road. The driver stopped the truck and some men got out. They were able to get within a few yards of the beast. Then it disappeared into the undergrowth.

The men had never seen an animal like it before. They decided that it must have been a "Wildman." For **centuries**, the Chinese have told tales of the Wildman. Like the yeti and Bigfoot, the Wildman is said to be big and covered with hair.

>> **valley** — The lower-lying land between hills or mountains

"Suddenly, the men saw a large, hairy figure...standing in the middle of the dirt road."

This is the valley of the great Chang (Yangtze) River. Many people think that its thick forests are home to the Wildman of China.

>> **centuries** — Hundreds of years

The woman in the center of this photograph is Gong Yulan. She is showing people the tree where she saw a Wildman in 1976.

After 1976, many other people reported seeing the Wildman. These reports came from the same area. The Chinese government decided to **investigate**.

Looking for Proof

Dr. Zhou Guoxing gathered together a team of scientists. For two years, the team searched through the forests of Hubei Province.

The team did not see a Wildman, but they found some huge footprints. They also gathered many descriptions of the creature from local people.

" (The Wildman) was scratching its back against a tree."

>> **investigate** — Try to find out all the facts

A woman named Gong Yulan said she had seen a hairy humanlike creature in 1976. It was scratching its back against a tree.

The scientists found some hairs on this tree. Experts examined these hairs. They said that the hairs were from an apelike animal. But they did not match the hairs of any known **species** of ape.

This Chinese poster shows a drawing of the Wildman. The writing on it says: "Have you seen the Wildman?"

Face-to-Face

The team heard an interesting story from a man named Pang Gensheng. He said he had met a Wildman while he was chopping wood.

For more than one hour, the Wildman and Gensheng stood looking at each other. Then Gensheng threw a stone at the beast's chest. It howled and ran away.

Gensheng said that this Wildman was about 7 feet (2 m) tall. It had long arms and a sloping forehead.

>> **species** — A group of animals that are so similar that they are able to breed

In 1961, road builders were working in a forest in Yunnan Province, China. They said they had killed a female Wildman, but it was smaller than the Wildman of Hubei Province. The workers said that the beast was only about 4 feet (1.2 m) tall.

A Smaller Wildman

There had also been reports of humanlike beasts on the Jiolong Mountain area of China. In 1957, some local people said they had killed a Wildman. One of them had kept the beast's hands and feet.

In 1980, Dr. Zhou Guoxing studied these hands and feet. He thought that they had come from a large and unknown type of monkey. Dr. Guoxing thought that the creature killed in Yunnan Province might have been one of these monkeys.

How Strange...

- Some ancient animal species still exist. These include the **tapir** and the giant panda.
- Both these animals are found in China. They are now in danger of dying out.

*Giant pandas have lived on Earth for about 600,000 years. A few still live in the mountains of central China. Could the Wildman of China be another **ancient** animal species that scientists thought had died out?*

>> **ancient** — Something from a very long time ago

The animals in the group at the right of this painting are Gigantopithecus apes. Maybe this creature is the real Wildman of China.

Giant Ape?

Dr. Guoxing began to think that there were two types of Wildman in China. One was about 6 feet (2 m) tall. The other was about 4 feet (1.2 m) tall.

About one million years ago, a giant species of ape lived in China. It is named *Gigantopithecus*. This ape was about 10 feet (3 m) tall. Scientists thought that it died out about 300,000 years ago.

Guoxing wondered if *Gigantopithecus* could still be living in Chinese forests. Could the larger Wildman be one of these apes? Or could it be something that is more like a modern human?

"Dr. Guoxing began to think that there were two types of Wildman..."

>> **tapir** — A piglike animal with hooves and a long, trunk-like nose

The Asian Almas

...Are wild people living in central Asia?

The lands of central Asia cover a large part of the world. There are tales of a hairy, humanlike beast living in and around this area. The creature is known as the Almas.

One of the strangest tales is of a female Almas named Zana. She was captured in the late 1800s. Zana had a large jaw, big teeth, and a flat nose. She never learned to talk.

Boris Porshnev was a Russian scientist. In 1964, he visited the village where Zana had lived. Porshnev found what he believed to be the skull of Zana's son. It looked like the skull of an ancient type of human known as **Neanderthal**.

Porshnev wrote about Zana. He suggested the Almas is a **survivor** of the Neanderthal people.

How Strange...

- Villagers told Porshnev that Zana's son had been very strong and difficult.
- Porshnev met one of Zana's grandsons. His jaw muscles were extremely strong. He could pick up a chair with a man in it, using his teeth.

>> **Neanderthal** — Early type of human that lived between 200,000 and 30,000 years ago

These are the Caucasus Mountains. They form the boundary between Asia and Europe. Many people claim to have seen the Almas there. The picture above is an artist's idea of what the Almas looks like.

>> **survivor** — One who continues to live after others in its group have died

There have been tales of the Almas for hundreds of years. In around 1910, a Russian scientist met with a **herdsman** from Kazakhstan in Central Asia. He told the scientist that he had watched a female Almas for several months.

"...the Almas screeched and bared her teeth when anyone went near her."

Strange Behavior

The herdsman said that the Almas screeched and bared her teeth when anyone went near her. She also slept in an odd position. She would rest on her knees and elbows with her forehead touching the ground. Her hands would be at the back of her neck. This Almas ate raw meat. Sometimes she ate vegetables and insects, too.

This is a Kazakh herdsman with his flock. Several herdsmen have claimed to have seen Almas while rounding up sheep.

>> **herdsman** — Someone who looks after a herd of animals

Hunting for Almas

Scientist Marie-Jeanne Koffman has spent many years investigating the Almas. She has collected hundreds of reports about them. Many people told her that they had seen the Almas in the Caucasus Mountains.

In one report, about 30 people had seen an Almas eating **corncobs** in a field. Koffman's team found a line of footprints in that field. They also found two Almas' caves. Inside, there were mounds of potatoes and fruits.

How Strange...

- Marie-Jeanne Koffmann found teethmarks on food in the Almas' caves. The jaws that had made them were wider than a human jaw.
- In 1984, Koffmann wrote that many villagers in the Caucasus lived in peace with the Almas. They would sometimes give food to the Almas.

Russian scientist Igor Burtsev is seen here with a cast of a giant footprint. The print was found in 1979.

>> **corncob** — The center part of an ear of corn on which the kernels grow

Neanderthal Survivors?

...Could the stories of humanlike beasts be linked to early humans?

Neanderthals were early humans that lived between 200,000 and 30,000 years ago. They are named for the Neander valley in Germany. The first ancient humanlike skeleton was discovered there in 1856.

Neanderthals had thick **browridges**, large teeth, and huge jaws. They had powerful bodies with large feet and hands. Until recently, scientists believed that Neanderthals had died out. They were followed by a different type of human. The later humans are known as the Cro-Magnons.

Today, some experts think that Neanderthals might have mixed and **interbred** with the Cro-Magnons. If the Neanderthals did not completely die out, then perhaps a few are still living in wild parts of the world.

>> **browridge** — Ridge, or raised area of bone, above the eyes

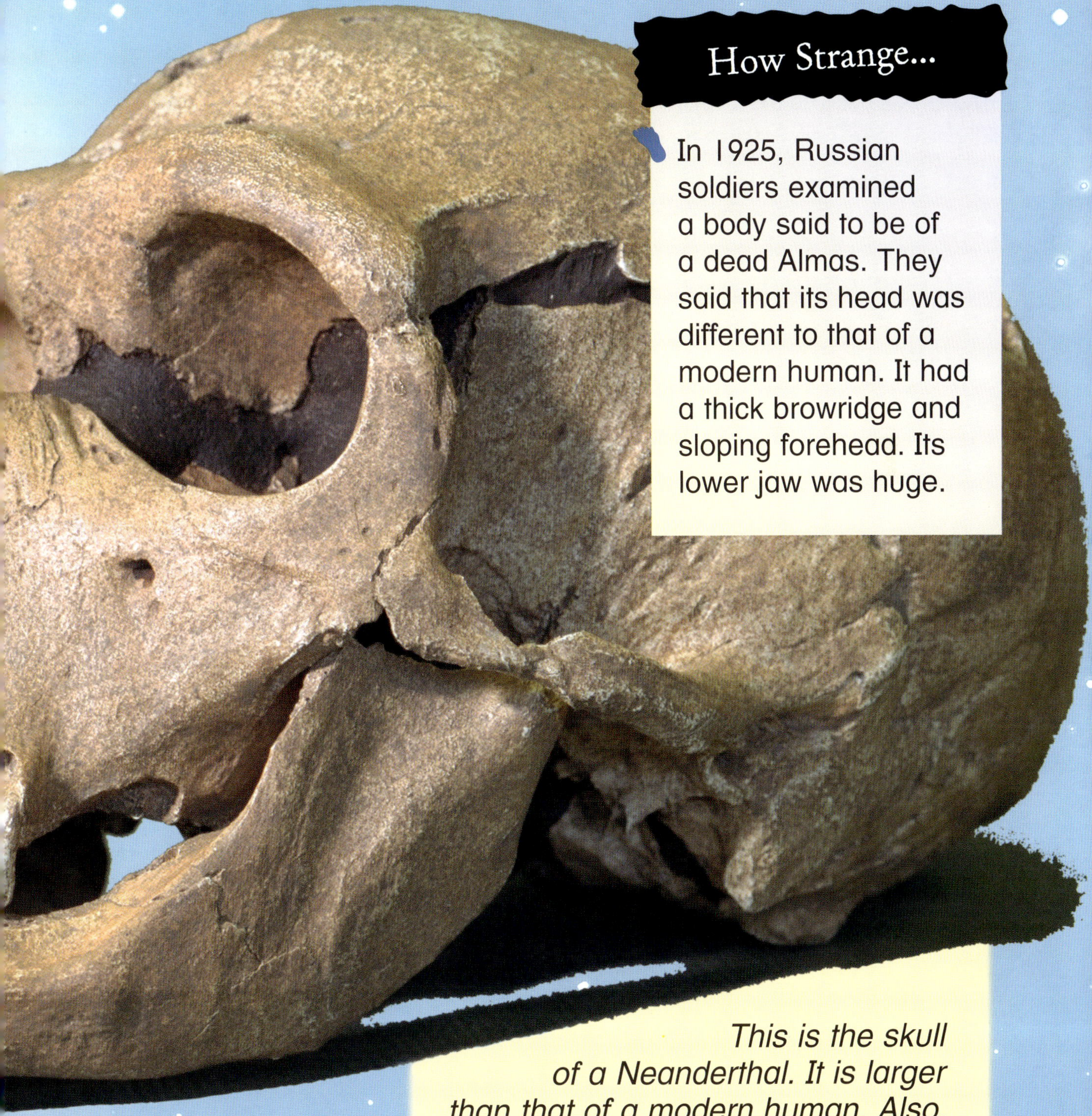

How Strange...

In 1925, Russian soldiers examined a body said to be of a dead Almas. They said that its head was different to that of a modern human. It had a thick browridge and sloping forehead. Its lower jaw was huge.

This is the skull of a Neanderthal. It is larger than that of a modern human. Also, the ridge above the eyes is thicker.

>> **interbred** — Produced children by mating with a different species, or type, of human

Neanderthal remains have been found in Europe, Asia, and along the North African coast. Because of this, we know that Neanderthals lived in these parts of the world.

Perhaps some giant humanlike creatures are Neanderthal survivors. But what about the North American Bigfoot? No Neanderthal remains have been found in North America.

This is an artist's idea of what a Neanderthal man looked like. Here he is shown hunting a rhinoceros.

Land Bridge

Millions of years ago, all the world's **continents** were joined together. Over time, the land broke up. The pieces drifted apart. In Neanderthal times, North America was still joined to Asia by a strip of land. This land bridge was across the Bering Strait. The Bering Strait is the narrow stretch of water that separates Alaska from Siberia in Russia.

Animals crossed over the land bridge. It is possible that some Neanderthals crossed from Asia to North America in the same way.

"Perhaps some giant humanlike creatures are Neanderthal survivors."

>> **continent** — One of seven large land masses on Earth

Vietnamese **Connection**?

In the 1960s, some U.S. marines said they had shot a huge ape in Vietnam. But there are no known large apes living there. Also, a Vietnamese man reported finding a hairy man sitting in a cave. Could these creatures have been Neanderthals?

No Neanderthal bones have been found in Vietnam. But it is possible that a surviving Neanderthal walked there from central Asia.

This map of the world roughly shows the areas where people have reported seeing giant humanlike beasts.

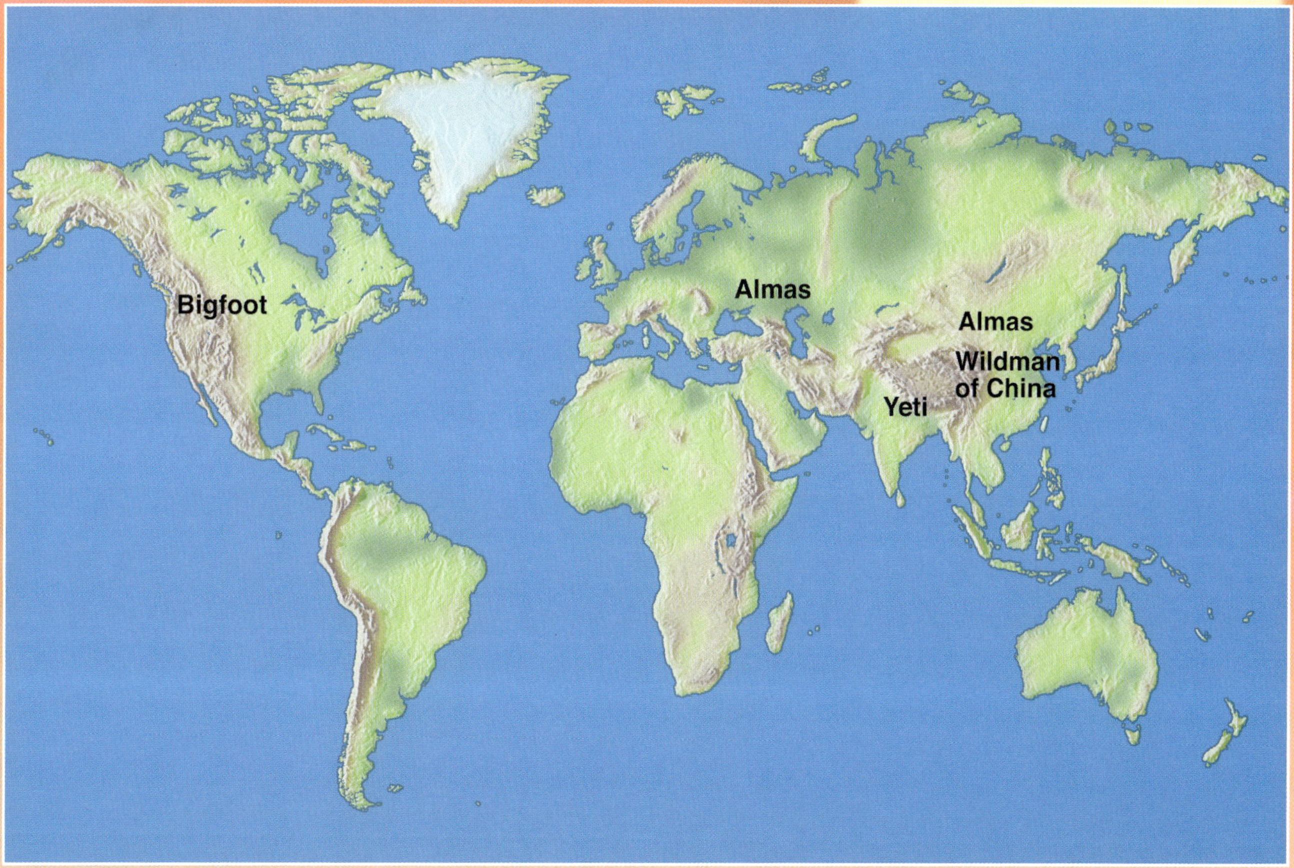

>> **connection** — The point where one thing is linked to another

Do giant humanlike creatures really exist? Some sightings could have been hoaxes. People could have imagined seeing them. Or they might be some **rare**, unknown creatures.

Proof Or Hoax?

In 1968, there was a report of a strange, apelike creature frozen into a block of ice. This creature was put on show. It became known as the Minnesota Iceman and people paid to see it.

Some scientists studied the Iceman through the block of ice. They believed that it was a real creature that had been shot dead. Later, the owner replaced it with a copy. Many people now believe that the Minnesota Iceman was a hoax.

The truck in this picture carries an advertisement for the Minnesota Iceman. At the top is a drawing of the creature inside the block of ice.

Shy Giants

Some scientists believe that a few Neanderthals still live in remote parts of the world. Many hunters have also felt sure of what they saw. They say they have seen shy, hairy creatures in wild places. Like humans, they walk on two feet.

>> **rare** — Uncommon and difficult to find

Glossary

ancient Something from a very long time ago

border A boundary or line that separates two countries or regions

browridge Ridge, or raised area of bone, above the eyes

centuries Hundreds of years

connection The point where one thing is linked to another

continent One of seven large land masses on Earth

corncob The central part of an ear of corn on which the kernels grow

herdsman Someone who looks after a herd of animals

hoax A trick

ice ax An ax used by mountaineers for cutting footholds in ice

interbred Produced children by mating with a different species, or type, of human

investigate Try to find out all the facts

kidnapped Taken away by force

logger A person who cuts down trees

Neanderthal Early type of human that lived between 200,000 and 30,000 years ago

peak The pointed top of a mountain or ridge

plaster cast Model made by pouring liquid plaster into a shape or mold, and letting it harden

rare Uncommon and difficult to find

remote A long way from cities or towns

snow-blind Blinded for a short time by the brightness of sunlight on snow

species A group of animals that are so similar that they are able to breed

summit The highest point of a mountain

survivor One who continues to live after others in its group have died

tapir A piglike animal with hooves and a long, trunk-like nose

undergrowth Bushes and plants growing under trees

valley The lower-lying land between hills or mountains, often with a river running through it

yak A long-haired ox found in Tibet and central Asia

Index

Further Reading

- Krensky, Stephen. *Bigfoot*, "Monster Chronicles" series. Lerner Publications, 2006.
- Shone, Rob. *Bigfoot and Other Strange Beasts*, "Graphic Mysteries" series. Rosen, 2006.
- Wallace, Holly. *The Mystery of the Abominable Snowman*, "Can Science Solve?" series. Heinemann, 2006.
- Woog, Adam. *Bigfoot*, "Mysterious Encounters" series. Kidhaven Press, 2006.